D1097465

Licensed exclusively to Top That Publishing Ltd
Tide Mill Way, Woodbridge, Suffolk, IP12 1AP, UK
www.topthatpublishing.com
Copyright © 2016 Tide Mill Media
All rights reserved
2 4 6 8 9 7 5 3 1
Manufactured in Zhejiang, China

Written by Oakley Graham
Illustrated by Natalie Smillie

ISBN 978-1-78700-269-2

A catalogue record for this book is available from the British Library

For my children, who make me happy and forget about my worries.—Oakley Graham

Rainbow Bird

Written by
Oakley Graham

Illustrated by
Natalie Smillie

Rainbow Bird lived in a very poor neighborhood on the outskirts of a large city. Rainbow Bird had the most beautiful singing voice and people would travel from miles around to listen to her song.

Rainbow Bird lived happily among the makeshift homes in the neighborhood. Although the people who lived there did not have much money, they loved Rainbow Bird's happy song and it made them forget about their worries.

One summer's day, as the hot sun was beating down, Rainbow Bird took a dust bath as she waited for a cool breeze to rise up from the valley below.

Suddenly, the cooler air that she had wished for whistled and moaned through the narrow alleys of the neighborhood and Rainbow Bird rejoiced, filling the air with birdsong.

As Rainbow Bird ruffled her feathers in the cooling breeze,
a dark shadow appeared...

Startled, Rainbow Bird prepared to take flight, but a large net blocked her escape.

In the blink of an eye, Rainbow Bird was captured!

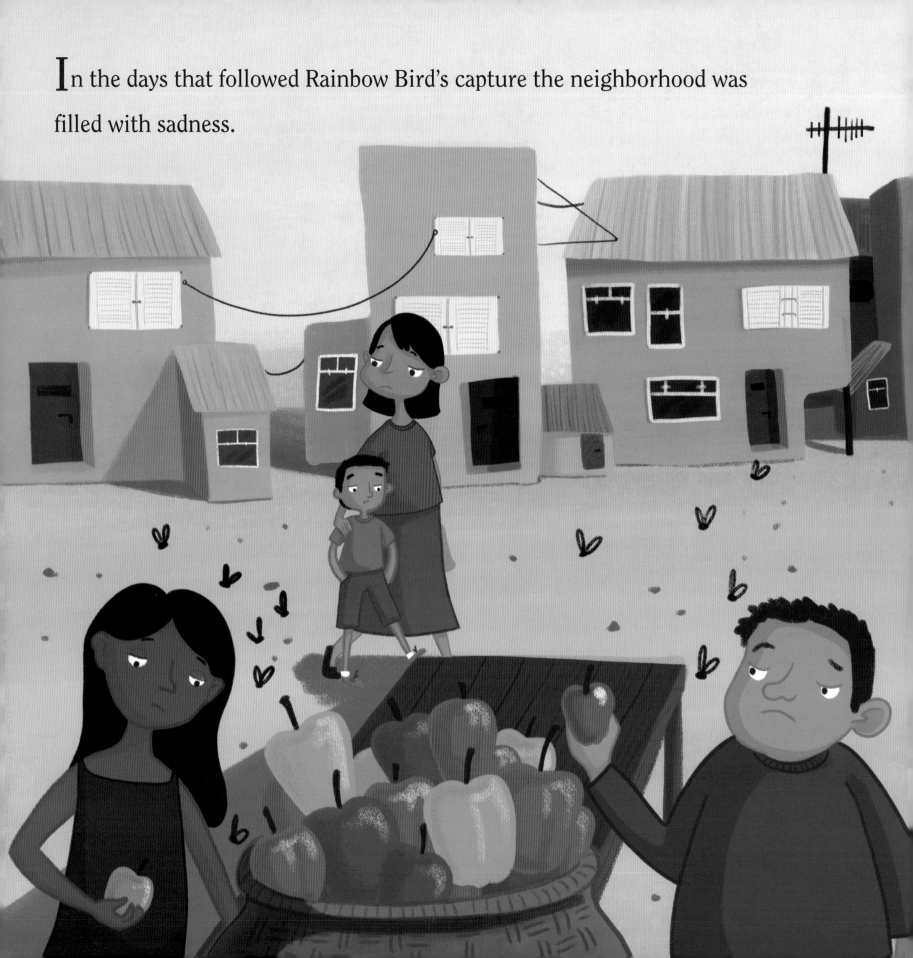

In the days that followed Rainbow Bird's capture the neighborhood was filled with sadness.

There was no happy birdsong to make people forget about their worries; only the annoying buzzing sound of flies that had made the neighborhood their home as well.

A young girl called Maria missed Rainbow Bird more than most.

Ever since Maria could remember, Rainbow Bird's happy melody had been a part of her life. When she was helping to look after her brothers and sisters or feeling sad, Rainbow Bird had seemed like her very own special little friend.

Maria could not stand the sadness of the neighborhood without Rainbow Bird's song to lift people's spirits, so she decided to go and look for her.

Maria had heard stories about bad people from the city who stole animals to sell.

So, she set off down the hillside towards the city on her search.

Maria walked and walked until the makeshift houses of her neighborhood gave way to the high-rise buildings of the city.

After hours of searching under the hot summer sun, Maria thought that she would never find her special little friend.

Then, as if in answer to her thoughts, Maria heard
Rainbow Bird's song drifting on the breeze.

Maria followed the birdsong and soon arrived at a shop.

The shop made Maria very angry! It was filled with exotic creatures that had been taken from the forest which surrounded the city...

...and Rainbow Bird!

Without pausing to think, Maria reached for Rainbow Bird's cage and unfastened the bolt.

Rainbow Bird took flight and Maria ran from the shop with tears of happiness running down her face.

Ducking down an alley, Maria paused to catch
her breath—she'd done it! She had found
Rainbow Bird and set her free!

Smiling, she started on the long walk back home.

It was night by the time Maria reached her home and she was tired, but very happy.

As she rested her sleepy head on the pillow, the air was filled with beautiful music.

Rainbow Bird's song filled the neighborhood with happiness once again.